Falkirk Council

Meadowbank Library

2a Stevenson Avenue

Polmont.

FK2 0GU

Bo'ness
01506 778520

Bonnybridge
01324 503295

Denny
01324 504242

Falkirk
01324 503605

Grangemouth
01324 504690

Larbert
01324 503590

Meadowbank
01324 503870

Slamannan
01324 851373

This book is due
for return on or
before the last date
indicated on the
label. Renewals
may be obtained
on application.

'Supernatural Summer Camp'
An original concept by Katie Dale
© Katie Dale 2024

Illustrated by Jared MacPherson

Published by MAVERICK ARTS PUBLISHING LTD
Suite 1, Hillreed House, 54 Queen Street,
Horsham, West Sussex, RH13 5AD
© Maverick Arts Publishing Limited September 2024
+44 (0)1403 256941

A CIP catalogue record for this book is available at the British Library.

ISBN 978-1-83511-036-2

Printed in India

Maverick
publishing
www.maverickbooks.co.uk

SUPERNATURAL SUMMER CAMP

Written by Katie Dale

Illustrated by Jared MacPherson

Chapter 1
Showbiz Summer Camp!

Sanjay's skin tingled with excitement as he packed his rucksack. For weeks he'd been counting down the days, the hours—even the minutes!—and tomorrow he was finally going to Showbiz Summer Camp in Whispering Woods!

Sanjay loved everything showbiz. He adored acting, dressing up, putting on different voices and, most of all, **MAGIC!** On the first night there was going to be a talent show, and Sanjay had spent ages preparing his homemade magician's cloak for his vanishing act! On one side, it looked like a normal black cloak, but the lining was stitched with hundreds of leaves...

One minute I'm here...

...the next, I'll disappear!

WHOOSH

SLSHH

Where've you gone? Bravo!

STLIIIITCH

PM 11:00

Sanjay stayed up late making sure everything was ready for his act...

...But he forgot to set his alarm clock!

Sanjay! Wake up! We're going to be late!

Sanjay quickly grabbed everything he needed...

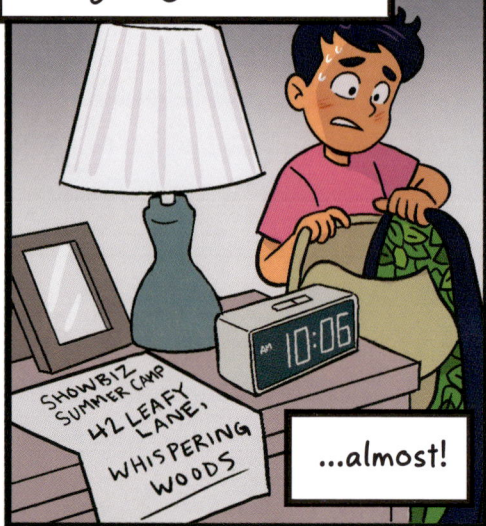

SHOWBIZ SUMMER CAMP
42 LEAFY LANE,
WHISPERING WOODS

...almost!

They drove as quickly as possible to Whispering Woods.

Which way now?

ROCKY ROAD
ELM STREET
LEAFY LANE
ACORN AVENUE

VRROOM!

I don't know! I left the address at home!

Look! That must be it! Quick! Everyone's already in costume for the talent show!

BLAH BLAH BLAH BLAH

Sanjay quickly changed into his magician's costume.

"Bye, Dad!" he called, grabbing his rucksack. "Will you find your way home okay?"

"Yes, of course!" his dad laughed. "I know *our* address—I'll just put it in the satnav! Have a wonderful time, Sanjay!"

"I will!" Sanjay waved as his dad drove away, then raced to join the other kids. Everyone's costumes were amazing! There were yetis and fairies and witches and ghosts! One of the ghost costumes looked so realistic it almost seemed see-through! *I wonder how that works?!* Sanjay thought enviously. *It would come in very handy for my magic vanishing act!* But just then, as he watched, the ghost drifted straight through a huge oak tree!

Sanjay froze. *How did he do that?!* The ghost passed through two more trees, then straight through a cabin wall! Sanjay's jaw dropped. His skin prickled as he looked around at everybody again. He suddenly had a funny feeling that *no one* was wearing costumes after all, and this *wasn't* Showbiz Summer Camp...

Sanjay desperately searched his rucksack for his mobile phone. *Please don't tell me I forgot that too!* he thought anxiously. He had to call his dad and get out of here—quickly!

Finally, Sanjay's fingers found his phone. *Yes!*

But he'd forgotten to charge it up! It was dead! *No!*

"No phones allowed at camp," said a stern voice.

Sanjay looked up and his eyes bulged. He was staring at a man who had the head, chest and arms of a human— but the body of a horse!

"Give it to me please, young vampire," the man-horse ordered.

Sanjay was startled and confused. *Vampire?!* Then suddenly he realised that his magician's cloak did look a bit like a vampire cape...

"B-but..." Sanjay stammered. "I-I'm not—"

"No buts!" the man-horse snapped, taking the phone.

Sanjay gulped. *Now* how would he get out of here?

And where on earth *was* he?!

Chapter 2
Not Showbiz Summer Camp!

Sanjay soon found out...

Welcome to Supernatural Summer Camp!

My name is Mr Hoof, and the first rule of camp is...

...avoid humans!

GULP!

Sanjay froze. There was no way he could tell Mr Hoof he was human now!

"No one from the human world can discover our existence," Mr Hoof continued, looking grim. "A single sighting or, worse still, a photograph of any of us, would threaten the entire supernatural community, globally."

Globally? Sanjay's eyes widened. Just how big was the supernatural community? Were there vampires and witches and werewolves hiding *everywhere?* He shuddered.

"If any of you so much as *smells* a human nearby, you must tell me *immediately*," Mr Hoof demanded, his expression dark, "and I will deal with them."

Sanjay gulped. He didn't like the sound of that! He suddenly really wished he'd had time for a shower that morning! He had to get out of here—quick! He pulled his cloak tighter and edged away from the group.

"Careful!" a nearby witch hissed, blocking his way. "You nearly stepped into that patch of sunlight!"

Sanjay frowned, confused. Why would that matter?

But of course! She thought he was a vampire and vampires burn in sunlight! Sanjay looked around miserably. There was no way he could get away from the group and back to the road without passing through sunlight and giving himself away! He'd *never* get out of here! Not in daylight, anyway...

"The second rule of camp..." Mr Hoof continued, "... is have fun!" He broke into a big smile. "Luckily, we have lots of wonderful activities to keep you entertained. First up: **UNICORN RACING!**"

Sanjay couldn't believe his ears. *Unicorns?! Unicorns were real?!* Suddenly he heard a whinny and spun round to see a herd of graceful white unicorns step out from between the trees, Sanjay gasped. Their manes

were so glossy and their swirly horns gleamed gold. They were the most beautiful creatures he'd ever seen!

Despite his nerves, Sanjay couldn't help but feel a tingle of excitement. Perhaps Supernatural Camp would actually be fun? After all, he couldn't escape until it got dark. Until then, he'd just have to try to blend in.

Sometimes blending in was easy...

Sometimes it wasn't!

Something wrong with your steak?

I'm vegetarian!

PEEEEELLL JUICE

Actually, I brought my own bottle of blood, thanks Amy!

Phew!

Yay! More steak for me!

13

Creepy, but surprisingly comfy!

SNOOOOOORRREEE

Now's my chance to escape...

CREEEAK

Eek!

So far, so good...

AHHHH!

Chapter 3
A Close Shave

Sanjay cowered, his heart hammering, eyes shut tight, bracing himself for the wolf to attack... but instead the wolf laughed!

"Sanjay," the wolf giggled. "It's me, Amy! Didn't you know I was a werewolf? And tonight's a full moon. Time to play!"

"Amy?" Sanjay blinked in shocked relief, unable to believe the petite girl he'd sat next to at dinner was now a gigantic wolf!

"Come and join us!" Amy laughed, bounding over to a pack of wolves in the trees. "It's a beautiful night."

"SANJAY!" a voice behind him cried suddenly.

Sanjay whirled around but couldn't see anyone.

"Up here!" the voice laughed, and Sanjay looked up just in time to see a witch called Wanda fly her broomstick straight across the full moon! "Would you like a ride?" she called.

Sanjay hesitated. If he didn't escape camp tonight he'd have to go a whole second day without anyone discovering he was human. But then, with the woods full of witches and werewolves, it would be very difficult to escape tonight after all. And riding a broomstick was kind of a once in a lifetime opportunity...

"Yes please!" he grinned, racing over as she gracefully landed in a clearing.

"It must be so nice for you to run around freely in the moonlight after having to stay out of the sun all day," Wanda said sympathetically as Sanjay climbed on behind her. "It must be so hard being a vampire."

"Um, yes it is." Sanjay bit his lip. He hated lying.

"Time to have some fun!" she grinned. **"ONE, TWO, THREE..."**

WHEEEEEEEEEE!
Woo-hoo! This is AMAZING!
Is this your first time flying?
Yes! It's incredible!
SPLASH
But don't you ever turn into a bat?
Uh-oh!
Um... no... I'm not old enough yet...
But...
Quick—I've got to go! The sun's coming up!
Phew!

The next day, everyone played tag in the woods...

TAG! You're it!

Can't catch me!

Grr, he's right—not without stepping into the sunlight and revealing I'm not a real vampire!

That's cheating, Yan!

But then...

OH NO!

Sanjay desperately waved his arms around and pointed at the approaching humans, but Yan just grinned and waved back at him, not understanding Sanjay's warning. He had no idea of the danger he was in!

Sanjay panicked. He had to do something, but what? He couldn't yell a warning, in case the humans heard him too—but he couldn't run into the sunny clearing to warn Yan without revealing that he wasn't a vampire!

He looked around quickly for someone to help—anyone else could run into the clearing and warn Yan, after all—but there was no one in sight. They'd all run away to avoid being tagged!

Sanjay's heart hammered as the humans got closer and closer... It could only be a matter of moments before one of them saw Yan and—**OH NO!**—the woman was carrying an enormous camera! If they took a photo of Yan, the whole supernatural community would be in danger!

There was only one thing for it.

Sanjay took a deep breath... and ran!

Chapter 4
The Vanishing Act

Sanjay, you're in sunlight!

As the humans approached, Sanjay thought fast...

"Hi!" Sanjay called, walking over to the couple, trying to stop them getting too close to Yan. "Beautiful day for a walk, isn't it?"

"Er yes!" the man replied. "But be careful. Did you hear that noise just now? It sounded like a bear."

"Oh no! That was me—I tripped over that log!" Sanjay forced a laugh as he lied. "I'm so clumsy! Besides, there aren't any bears in these woods!"

"Are you sure?" the woman frowned. "We thought we saw a glimpse of one earlier..."

"Absolutely positive!" Sanjay laughed. "I've lived in these woods all my life—there are definitely no bears! It must have been a dog, that's all! There are lots of dog-walkers!"

The couple looked at each other uncertainly.

"But if it's rare wildlife you're looking for," Sanjay continued hastily, "a family of beavers were recently re-introduced to the river on the other side of the woods. The babies are so cute when they splash in the water!"

"Really? How amazing!" the woman gasped, beaming.

"Come on, darling! I can't wait to see those beaver kits!"

"Thank you very much!" the man grinned at Sanjay as they hurried away.

"You're welcome!" Sanjay called, breathing a sigh of relief as they disappeared from sight. "You can come out, Yan!" he hissed. "They've gone."

Yan peeked out nervously from under the leaf cloak.

"That was so close!" he said, his face pale. "The humans would have seen me for sure, if you hadn't hidden me!"

Sanjay nodded.

"But Sanjay... you're standing in sunlight..." Yan continued slowly, staring at him wide-eyed. "Doesn't that mean..."

"I'm not a vampire," Sanjay confessed, sighing heavily. "I'm human. I came to Supernatural Camp by accident, but I guess I'll have to leave now my secret's out," he said sadly. "It's been the best time of my life, meeting you all!"

Yan frowned. Then he heaved a huge sigh. Then, to Sanjay's surprise... he gave him an enormous hug!

"It's all my fault!" he cried. "I'm so sorry I cheated at tag!"

You risked everything to save me! You're the best human I've ever met! Don't go! Your secret's safe with me!

But it wasn't secret for long...
Get back to camp! You've both got a lot of explaining to do!
!!!
!!!
WHIRL
UH-OH!

Chapter 5
Facing The Music

"Yan!" Mr Hoof yelled, back at camp. "What on earth were you thinking, dancing around in that clearing? You put yourself at risk. You put us *all* at risk! You were almost seen!"

Yan's shoulders slumped miserably. "I'm so sorry, Mr Hoof," he sighed. "I'll never be that careless again. But please don't blame Sanjay, it was all my—"

"I will deal with Sanjay next," Mr Hoof snapped. "Go back to your cabin."

Yan looked at Sanjay apologetically as he slumped out the door. Sanjay sighed heavily. That was probably the last time he'd see Yan or any of his supernatural friends ever again.

"I'm s-so sorry, Mr Hoof," Sanjay stammered.

"I never meant to come to Supernatural Camp or to lie to you all. But when you thought I was a vampire and then told everyone to all avoid contact with humans, I was so scared I *couldn't* tell you the truth... and then I started having so much fun with you all I didn't *want* to tell you the truth," he admitted. "I'm really very sorry." Sanjay stared at the floor. "I promise I won't tell anyone about any of you."

"I know you won't," Mr Hoof replied.

Sanjay gulped. What did *that* mean? What was Mr Hoof going to do to him to make sure their secret stayed secret? Exile him to the depths of Siberia? Lock him in a dungeon? Make one of the witches cast a horrible spell on him?

"Sanjay..." Mr Hoof said slowly. "In my experience, humans cannot be trusted. They don't understand supernatural beings. They're scared of us. And humans tend to hunt and capture any creature they're scared of, and any being that is unlike themselves."

Sanjay closed his eyes, bracing himself for the worst.

But you have proven yourself to be an exception.

Wait, what?!

You risked your own safety to keep our secret. You have proven we can trust you.

You mean... I can stay?!

Of course! The supernatural community owes you huge thanks. How can we ever repay you?

Um... actually, there is one thing...

29

Could I please have some vegetarian food? I'm starving!

Of course!

Sanjay hadn't thought Supernatural Camp could get any better...

...but now he could finally be himself, it was perfect.

FLAP FLAP FLAP

TA-DA!

Wow! Where's Yan gone?!

That's magic!

Are you *sure* you're not supernatural?

When it was finally time to leave, Sanjay sadly hugged his supernatural friends goodbye.

"I'll never forget you all!" he promised.

"We'll never forget you either, Sanjay!" Wanda sniffed. "I'm so glad you accidentally came to Supernatural Camp!"

"Me too!" Sanjay said, smiling.

"Me three!" cried Yan. "By the way, I forgot to ask: which camp did you *mean* to go to?"

"Showbiz Camp!" Sanjay grinned. "I love magic and acting!"

"Well, you've certainly had a magical summer!" Amy laughed. "And you're by far the best actor I've ever seen!"

Sanjay laughed, then sighed. "I'll miss you all so much."

"It's only twelve months!" Mr Hoof chuckled.

Sanjay blinked. "You mean... I can come back next year?"

Mr Hoof grinned. "It wouldn't be the same without you!"

"Hurray!" Sanjay cheered, just as his dad's car arrived.

"Did you have fun at camp?" Sanjay's dad asked.

"IT WAS THE BEST SUMMER EVER!" Sanjay beamed. "So far!"

The End

WHAT NEXT?

Did you enjoy this Fusion Reader? If you are looking for more, the Maverick Reading Scheme is a bright, attractive range of books with plenty of stories for everyone. All titles are book-banded for guided reading to the industry standard and edited by a leading educational consultant.

MAVERICK FUSION READERS

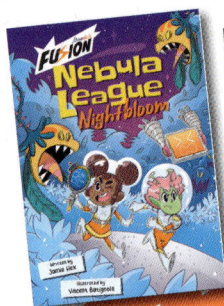

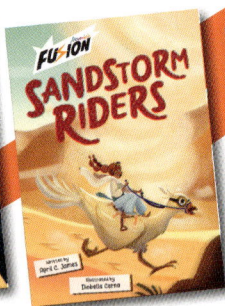

To view the whole Maverick Reading Scheme, visit our website at

www.maverickearlyreaders.com

Or scan the QR code to view our scheme instantly!